# The Daddy Longlegs Blues

By Mike Ornstein

Illustrated by Lisa Kopelke

Daddy Long Legs BLUES

Daddy Long Legs BLUES Tonight!

STERLING

New York / London

STERLING and the distinctive Sterling logo
are registered trademarks of Sterling Publishing Co., Inc.

Library of Congress Cataloging-in-Publication Data

Ornstein, Mike.
    The Daddy Longlegs blues / Mike Ornstein ; illustrated by Lisa Kopelke.
        p. cm.
    Summary: Daddy Longlegs, a blues musician in a backyard boogie-woogie band, shim-
mies through the cool grass, glides across the swimming pool, relaxes beside the waterspout, and preens his eight legs before the big concert.
    ISBN 978-1-4027-4359-7
    [1. Daddy longlegs--Fiction. 2. Blues (Music)--Fiction. 3. Musicians--Fiction. 4. Stories
in rhyme.] I. Kopelke, Lisa, ill. II. Title.

PZ8.3.O735Dad 2008                                          2007001772
[E]--dc22

10   9   8   7   6   5   4   3   2   1

Published by Sterling Publishing Co., Inc.
387 Park Avenue South, New York, NY 10016
Text © 2009 by Mike Ornstein
Illustrations © 2009 Lisa Kopelke
Distributed in Canada by Sterling Publishing
% Canadian Manda Group, 165 Dufferin Street
Toronto, Ontario, Canada M6K 3H6
Distributed in the United Kingdom by GMC Distribution Services
Castle Place, 166 High Street, Lewes, East Sussex, England BN7 1XU
Distributed in Australia by Capricorn Link (Australia) Pty. Ltd.
P.O. Box 704, Windsor, NSW 2756, Australia

Printed in China

Sterling ISBN 978-1-4027-4359-7

The paintings in the book were created using
acrylic & color pencil on Crescent Cold Press illustration board

For information about custom editions, special sales, premium
and corporate purchases, please contact Sterling Special Sales Department
at 800-805-5489 or specialsales@sterlingpublishing.com.

TICKET 3541

For my Momma
& my Daddy
—M.O.

To my big Daddy
Longlegs & my little
Love Bug
—L.K.

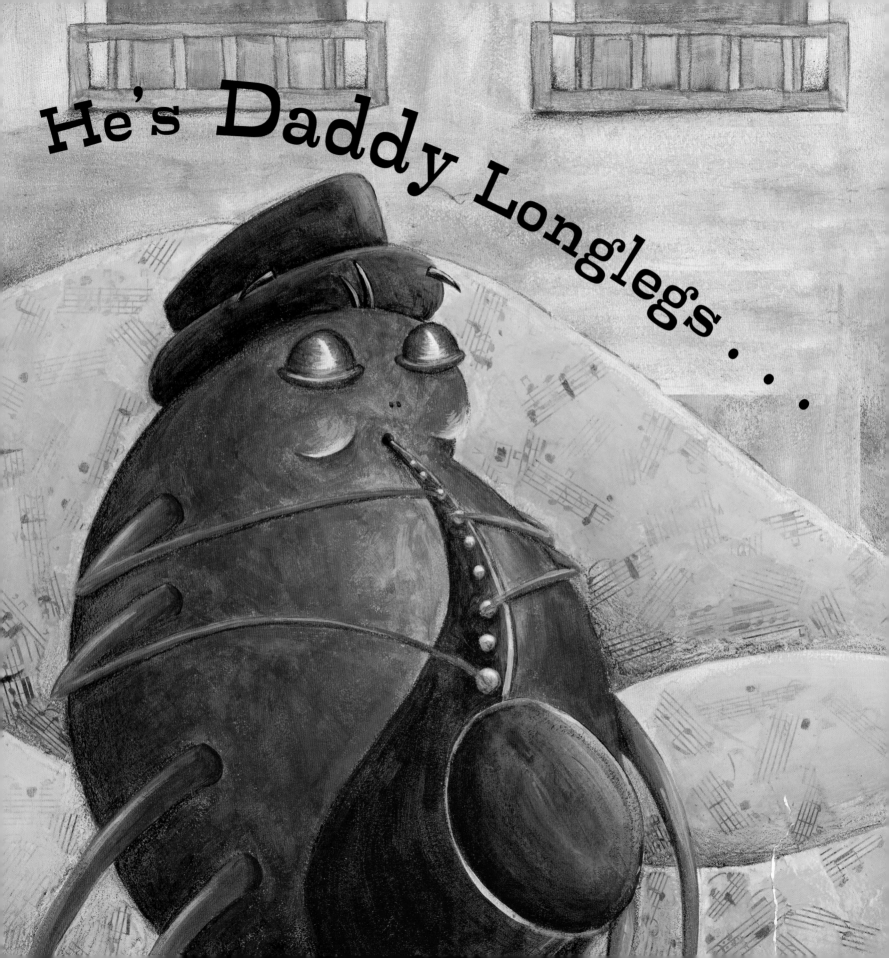

He digs dank, dark spaces.

He brings rhythm and soul to gloomy places.

Just get mellow to the bellow of his saxophone.

He's the world's most rhythmical opilione.

He plays the blues.

The Daddy Longlegs Blues.

He can't spin a web
  like those fancy spiders do.
His daddy was a wanderer
  and his momma was, too.
He hatched from an egg
  his momma laid in a crack
just before she got squashed
  in the back of a shack.

He has the blues.

# The Daddy
# Longlegs Blues.

**Bounce** with The Daddy as he plays his fiddle. He's eight long legs with a dot in the middle.

He's Daddy Longlegs, always on the move.

Glidin' over grass to his slow-motion groove.

Not a hurry or a worry, just playin' it cool.

Dancin' cross the water of the swimming pool.

Well, don't call him a spider!
Don't you call him no bug!
A bug could never give you an eight-legged hug.

He's Daddy Longlegs, and he'll do you no harm.
He tickles as he touches when he's
crawlin' up your arm.

Shake your booty
with The Daddy as he
strums on his bass.

He's got sunglasses on
and a grin on his face.

# He's Daddy Longlegs,

and when the sun comes out,
he'll rest his weary legs beside a waterspout.
Hang loose with The Daddy as he falls asleep
while his long lazy legs make his guitar weep.
**He has the blues.**
**He has the Lazy Legs Blues.**

He has eight long legs but he ain't got feet.

He'll **SCAt** across your ceiling . . .

. . . and get **FUnKy** on your floor.

ShAKe his booty down your hallway
and then ShiMmY out the door.

Just look at him go, **bouncin'** and a **boppin'**.

Creepin'
and a crawlin',
**no stop,
stop,
stoppin'.**

He's Daddy Longlegs,
roamin' all through the night.
Huntin' little bugs in the pale moonlight.

A sip of muddy water's all The Daddy needs to keep his boogie groovin' through the grass and weeds.

Do the boogie with The Daddy all across the land, as he plays the boogie-woogie on his baby grand.

He plays the blues.
The Boogie-Woogie Blues.

It's Daddy Longlegs, about to make the scene,
preenin' his long legs to keep them nice and clean.

So when you see The Daddy comin', better pay him his dues.
He's a rambler and a legend with

# The Daddy Longlegs Blues.

# GLOSSARY OF
# BLUES TERMS

Baby Grand: the smallest size of the grand piano.

Boogie-Woogie: a particular style of blues piano played fast and funky.

Dig: to understand or appreciate something.

Funky: having the soulful feeling of early blues.

Groove: a steady rhythmic pattern or an enjoyable listening experience.

Muddy Waters: the famous blues musician dubbed "King of Chicago Blues," Muddy Waters is credited for shifting the rural acoustic blues to the electric urban blues in the late 1940s.

Rambler: someone who moves from place to place, never settling down.

Scat: when a singer improvises nonsense syllables and imitates the sounds produced by instruments.

Shimmy: a dance done by wiggling one's shoulders back and forth.

Soul: expressing deep feeling or emotion.

# MUSICAL INSTRUMENTS
## PLAYED BY DADDY LONGLEGS

**Fiddle:** a violin used to play bluegrass or folk music, often refitted with all metal strings and a tuner on each string.

**Bass guitar:** a four to six string fretted instrument, generally tuned an octave lower than the guitar.

**Guitar:** a string instrument from Spain, with a large flat-backed sound box, violin-like curved shape, a fretted neck and six strings. It is played by strumming, plucking, or picking the strings.

**Saxophone:** in the woodwind family, a group of brass instruments with conical tubes and finger keys, having single-reed, clarinet-type mouthpieces.

**Drum:** percussion instrument made up of stretched skin or membrane over a cylinder. When you hit the top of the drum and create a rhythmic vibration.

**Piano:** a keyboard instrument. Sound is produced when a hammer strikes a string when one of the piano's eighty-eight keys are pressed.

# DADDY LONGLEGS and the BLUES

Like many blues players, Daddy Longlegs are ramblers, wandering through life to their own funky rhythm.

There are three different creatures that people call Daddy Longlegs—the adult crane fly, the cellar spider, and the more popular harvestman. Our Daddy Longlegs hero, a harvestman, isn't a spider, or even an insect! Harvestmen belong to a different order known as Opiliones, but they are often mistaken for spiders because they've got eight long legs. Unlike spiders, harvestmen do not produce silk or spin webs. They have no fangs, two eyes instead of eight, and they appear to have only one central body part—that's the "dot in the middle." They are harmless to people, but they eat smaller insects, plants, and fungi. They spend a lot of time cleaning or "preening" their legs, probably so they're in top form to jam with a funky backyard blues band! Farmers began calling them harvestmen because they appeared in the fields during harvest time.

Like the Daddy Longlegs in the field, blues music crept on the scene during the late nineteenth century in the Mississippi Delta. The blues grew out of the sad songs of slaves working in the fields, and became a way for people to tell their life's story through music. In time, blues music influenced the creation of jazz, rock, soul, R&B, and hip-hop. Many blues songs express feelings of sadness and loss, but ideally, playing and singing the blues is a way to *cure* you from feeling blue. There are also happy, upbeat songs called jump blues. Either way—happy or sad—blues music represents life. When people—or Daddy Longlegs—sing the blues, they are singing about being alive.